LOOK WHAT THE CAT DRAGGED IN!

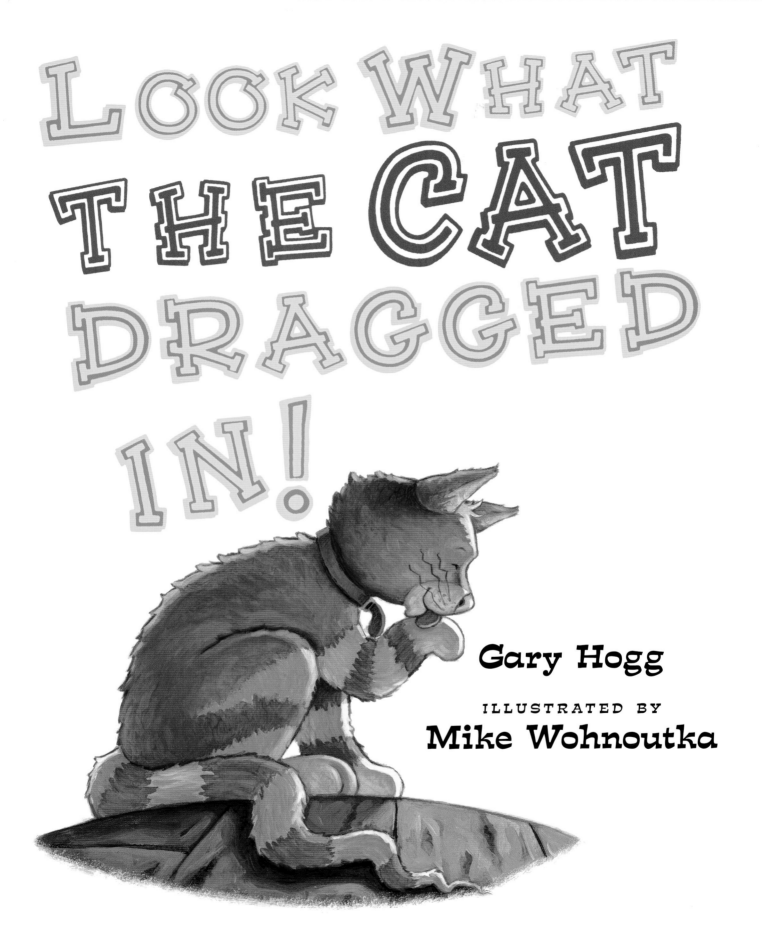

Gary Hogg

ILLUSTRATED BY
Mike Wohnoutka

Dutton Children's Books ⊙ New York

DUTTON CHILDREN'S BOOKS
A division of Penguin Young Readers Group

Published by the Penguin Group
Penguin Group (USA) Inc, 375 Hudson Street, New York, New York 10014, U.S.A. · Penguin Group
(Canada), 10 Alcorn Avenue, Toronto, Ontario, Canada M4V 3B2 (a division of Pearson Penguin
Canada Inc.) · Penguin Books Ltd, 80 Strand, London WC2R 0RL, England · Penguin Ireland, 25 St
Stephen's Green, Dublin 2, Ireland (a division of Penguin Books Ltd) · Penguin Group (Australia), 250
Camberwell Road, Camberwell, Victoria 3124, Australia (a division of Pearson Australia Group Pty
Ltd) · Penguin Books India Pvt Ltd, 11 Community Centre, Panchsheel Park, New Delhi—110 017,
India · Penguin Group (NZ), Cnr Airborne and Rosedale Roads, Albany, Auckland 1310, New Zealand
(a division of Pearson New Zealand Ltd) · Penguin Books (South Africa) (Pty) Ltd, 24 Sturdee
Avenue, Rosebank, Johannesburg 2196, South Africa · Penguin Books Ltd, Registered Offices:
80 Strand, London WC2R 0RL, England

CIP Data is available.

Published in the United States by Dutton Children's Books,
a division of Penguin Young Readers Group
345 Hudson Street, New York, New York 10014
www.penguin.com/youngreaders

Designed by Richard Amari

Manufactured in China · First Edition
1 3 5 7 9 10 8 6 4 2
ISBN 0-525-46984-2

For my sisters, Kathy, Debbie, Linda, Sally, Paula, and Verda Rae.
Not a lazybones in the bunch.
G.H.

For my wife, Anna, and our son, Franklin
M.W.

Deep in the woods, the winter wind whipped and
swirled around Lazybone Cabin.

The family stared into the fireplace, watching the last piece of firewood burn.

"Now it's cold," said Grandma Lazybones. "My teeth are going to chatter."

"I hear you," said Daddy Lazybones. "My feet are frosty already."

Junior sneezed.

"Did you hear that? Junior's got the sniffles," said Mama Lazybones. The family turned and eyed the little cat, sleeping on the floor.

"They say a catskin quilt is the best way to keep the chill off," said Grandma.

"Of course, there's nothing like kitty-fur slippers when you want toasty tootsies," said Daddy Lazybones.

Mama shifted in her seat. "And this chair is too hard. Why can't I have a fluffy cat pillow?"

"Forget that!" boomed Junior. "Get me a cat hat before my ears freeze off!"

The little cat cracked open the back door and
sneaked out.

Shortly, the front door flew open. In came the cat, dragging a sled piled high with firewood.

"Hot dog!" Grandma Lazybones chuckled. "Look what the cat dragged in!"

Daddy Lazybones put wood in the fireplace and set it ablaze. The fire burned brightly, and soon the cabin was warm again.

Soon enough, Lazybone Cabin fell silent. Grandma rocked. Daddy scratched. Mama stared off into space. Junior twiddled his thumbs. And the little cat curled up and went to sleep.

By and by, a terrible growl rumbled through the room.

"Sounds like a wolf," said Daddy Lazybones.

"That's no wolf," barked Grandma Lazybones. "It's my stomach. I'm nearly starved to death, and there's not so much as a crumb to eat."

The family turned and eyed the little sleeping cat.

"Of course," said Grandma, leaning over, "I was never one to pass up a tasty kitty-cat casserole."

"Then again, a hot bowl of cream-of-cat soup always hits the spot," said Mama Lazybones.

Daddy Lazybones smacked his lips. "If you ask me, nothing beats a kitty kebab with all the fixin's."

"I want a peanut butter and cat sandwich!" bawled Junior.

The little cat yanked open the back door and slipped out.

Shortly, the front door flew open. In came the cat, dragging a sled piled high with take-out food.

"Oh goody," Mama Lazybones sang out. "Look what the cat dragged in!"

The Lazybones slurped and burped and gobbled every morsel in record time.

Soon enough, Lazybone Cabin fell silent. Grandma rocked. Daddy scratched. Mama stared off into space. Junior twiddled his thumbs. And the little cat curled up and went to sleep.

Eventually, Junior Lazybones let loose a huge sigh and whined, "I'm bored."

"Now, Junior," said Daddy Lazybones, "there must be something we could do."

The family turned and eyed the little sleeping cat.

"Pin the tail on the cat is always fun," said Mama Lazybones.

"In my day, we'd go for a kittyback ride," said Grandma.

"How about an old-fashioned game of kitty Ping-Pong?" suggested Daddy Lazybones.

"Let's dog-pile on the cat!" hollered Junior.

The little cat flung open the back door and scampered out.

Shortly, the front door flew open. In came the cat, dragging a sled piled high with toys and games of every kind.

"Hooray!" Junior cheered. "Look what the cat dragged in!"

The Lazybones laughed and laughed, playing one game after another.

Soon enough, Lazybone Cabin fell silent. Grandma rocked. Daddy scratched. Mama stared off into space. Junior twiddled his thumbs. And the little cat curled up and went to sleep.

"I've been thinking," said Daddy Lazybones, breaking the silence. "All we do around here is work, work, work."

"That's the truth," said Mama. "With a load of money, we could take it easy for a change."

The family turned and eyed the little sleeping cat.

"Rich people pay top dollar for kitty-cat doormats," said Grandma Lazybones.

"Cowboys love cat ropin'!" exclaimed Mama Lazybones. "That's where the money is."

"Or grizzly-bear bait," said Daddy Lazybones. "With big-game hunters, you can name your own price."

"Sell him to the circus to be a flying-cat cannonball!" Junior roared.

The little cat threw open the back door and dashed out.

Shortly, the front door flew open. In came the cat, dragging a
sled piled high with bags of money.

"Yippee!" hollered Daddy Lazybones. "Look what the cat dragged in!"

"We're rich!" whooped Mama Lazybones. "This tattered rug has got to go."

"That lazy cat, too," added Grandma Lazybones.

"Let's buy a dog!" Junior shouted.
The little cat jerked open the back door and stomped out.

Shortly, the front door flew open.

In came the cat, dragging a sled piled high with a woodsman, a chef, a toy maker, a banker, and a policeman.

"Yikes!" shouted Daddy Lazybones. "Look what the cat dragged in!"

"Thieves!" bellowed the woodsman.

"Criminals!" cried the chef.

"Crooks!" snapped the toy maker.

"Robbers!" yelled the banker.

They chased the Lazybones around and around the cabin.
A piece of firewood bonked Daddy Lazybones on the head.
Grandma fell into the take-out trash. Mama tripped on a bag of
money. Junior got tangled in the yo-yo string.

The policeman hauled the Lazybones to jail.
Lazybone Cabin fell silent.

And the little cat curled up and went to sleep on its tattered
little rug on the hard floor.
Smiling.